ISBN 0-86163-803-4

Copyright © 1975 Award Publications Limited

Published by Award Publications Limited,
1st Floor, 27 Longford Street,
London, NW1 3DZ

Printed in Italy

Roddy in the Rain

by Rene Cloke

AWARD PUBLICATIONS LIMITED

RODDY IN THE RAIN

Roddy Rabbit had a new red mackintosh and a pair of rubber boots and he was just longing for a rainy day.

He stood on the doorstep one morning and looked at the sky; it was blue and the sun was shining. But what was that? He felt several drops of water on his head!

He looked up and saw his sister, Ruth, watering the plants in her window-box.

"Lovely day!" she called out.

The next day was better, although no one but Roddy thought so. There were heavy black clouds overhead and, by mid-day, the rain was coming down beautifully. It ran down the window-panes and collected in little pools on the garden path. Drip, drip, it fell from the eaves and splash, splash, onto the ground.

Lovely rain!

"Old Mrs Bunnyfluff at Heather Warren has asked us to go to tea with her this afternoon," Ruth reminded Roddy.

"I shall start early and walk there," said Roddy. "It's a splendid afternoon for a walk."

Ruth said she would catch the bus and meet him at Mrs Bunnyfluff's gate.

Roddy trudged along in the rain, walking in all the puddles. In his red mackintosh and rubber boots he was quite, quite dry.

"Hello, Roddy!" called Jerry Jay as he passed by. "Are you on your way to the birthday party?"

"Oh, no," said Roddy. "I'm going to tea with Mrs Bunnyfluff at Heather Warren."

"Mrs Bunnyfluff is giving a birthday party," replied Jerry, who always seemed to know everything. "I've seen several rabbits who are going there and they are all taking birthday presents."

"We didn't know it was her birthday," said Roddy. "What a good thing I met you. Thank you for letting me know."

He hurried along, planning to call at the village shop, but when he got there the door was locked.

There were such a lot of nice things in the window that would have been just right for Mrs Bunnyfluff's birthday present—fancy tins of biscuits, kettle holders, pincushions and pretty little egg-cups with cosies to match.

Roddy tapped on the door but there was no answer.

It was early closing day.

Roddy felt very worried as he went on his way. He did not like to arrive at a birthday party without a present and he felt sure that Ruth would be upset.

"Well, I can't make a present out of nothing," he said.

Then he decided he would go through the wood and see if he could pick a bunch of flowers for Mrs Bunnyfluff.

"Better than nothing," he thought, "and I'll take a proper present another day."

But although Roddy searched the woods there were not many flowers to pick. A few weeks ago the banks had been full of prim-roses, but now they were nearly over and those that were left were rather spattered with mud.

Roddy gathered a little bunch with a few violets and two early bluebells, then he added a spray of hazel catkins and wandered on, hoping to find something else.

He met some of his squirrel friends. They tried to be helpful and kindly offered him some nuts from their store-room, but Roddy was sure that old Mrs Bunnyfluff would not want nuts.

Mark and Margery Magpie showed him a piece of silver paper from their treasure hoard. "It's probably quite valuable," said Mark. "There is not so much of it left about in the road as there used to be."

"Thank you," said Roddy, "but I don't think Mrs Bunnyfluff is very much interested in silver paper."

A rather stupid hedgehog, who was poking about amongst the dead leaves, suggested that Roddy should pick a basketful of blackberries to take to Mrs Bunnyfluff. When Roddy pointed out that it was not the right time of year for blackberries, the hedgehog replied that if he was not going to take advice he ought not to ask for it and went on shuffling the leaves.

He had gone rather a long way into the woods, so he decided to cross the stream by the stepping-stones and make his way up to the road again.

The stream was burbling along almost like a little river and Roddy, in his rubber boots, found it difficult to keep his balance on the stepping-stones.

Half-way across he nearly fell over—wobble, wobble. He just managed to save himself, but he dropped the bunch of flowers and they went drifting away in the swirling water.

Roddy reached the other bank safely and
scrambled up the muddy path through the
trees to the road.

"Why, I hadn't noticed it had stopped
raining," he said in surprise, as he rubbed
his muddy boots on the grass and brushed a
few twigs and dry leaves from his red mackintosh.

The sun was just breaking through the clouds as a little blue car drew up at the side of the road.

"Can I give you a lift?" cried Hubert Hare. "Which way are you going?"

"Thank you," said Roddy. "I think I've walked far enough, and I shall be late for Mrs Bunnyfluff's party if I walk all the way to Heather Warren."

He climbed in beside Hubert and told him all about the birthday party.

"The shop was shut so I couldn't buy a birthday present," he explained. "I tried to pick a bunch of flowers in the woods but there were not many left. Those I did get, I dropped as I was crossing the stream."

"That's a sad story," agreed Hubert, "but I've got an idea. There is a Fair at Heather Warren and there will be all sorts of pretty things on the stalls—vases and brooches, fountain pens and necklaces. Perhaps you might be lucky enough to win something for a birthday present."

"That would be splendid!" gasped Roddy. "Do you think there will be time to go there?"

"Just a quick visit," said Hubert, and the little car bowled along towards Heather Warren.

The Fair was very merry. All the stall keepers were delighted that the rain had stopped just in time for the fun to begin.

There were roundabouts and swing-boats and all kinds of side-shows where curious and wonderful things could be seen.

The pictures outside the tents showed jugglers
and tight-rope walkers, funny clowns and con-
jurors. Everything looked very exciting and
it was difficult not to stop.

Roddy and Hubert made their way through
the crowd, past stalls where tickets were being
sold for lucky numbers; but Roddy could not
wait for this.

There were roars and cheers for those who swung a hammer and rang a bell, and for those who were able to shoot and hit little balls that were tossed into the air on jets of water.

Then they came to a stall where toys, vases and boxes of chocolates could be won. You had to be very clever and throw a wooden ring over the thing you wanted.

Roddy looked at the stall
and decided that a pretty
blue vase would be just right
for Mrs Bunnyfluff.

"I'll have six
rings," he said.

"That's right,
sir! Best of
luck!" said the
stall keeper,
handing him the
rings.

Roddy was usually rather good at games, but perhaps he was in too much of a hurry. Somehow the rings would not go over the blue vase.

Again and again he tried, with Hubert and the stall keeper encouraging him.

"Just a little higher!"

"More to the right!"

"Hard luck, sir!"

"I'll have six more rings," he said," and then I must go. Ruth will be so cross if I'm late."

"Steady does it!" warned Hubert.

"Off you go!" cried the stall keeper.

Roddy threw more carefully this time, and the last ring looked as though it would win the vase. But no! It tipped over and went right around a little toy engine instead!

"Oh, bother!" cried Roddy. "That's not a bit of good for old Mrs Bunnyfluff. It would be a silly present to give her; but I can't wait any longer." And taking the little engine he hurried over to the Warren.

Ruth was waiting at Mrs Bunnyfluff's gate, looking very worried.

"It's a birthday party!" she whispered to Roddy as he came running up to her. "Mrs Bunnyfluff has her little grandson staying with her and it's his birthday. Sally Lopears told me in the bus, but, of course, it was too late to buy a present then."

"Her little grandson's birthday?" laughed Roddy. "Why, that's splendid!"

He showed Ruth the toy engine.

"How lucky that I didn't win the blue vase, after all!"

Mrs Bunnyfluff's grandson was delighted with the little engine and felt quite certain that Roddy, in his red mackintosh, must be Father Christmas.

"And after the party, I'll take you to spend the evening at the Fair," said Ruth. "That shall be *my* birthday present."